Live Green everyday for your Earth and your future!

[illegible]
Green Wise Kids
Author/Illustrator

Christmas 2011

The author of this book was in the audience of a presentation I was making at the University of Wisconsin Riverfalls. She gave me a book.

Love,
Grandpa
Gary

Author & Illustrator
Jean A. Gagnon Clausen

Contributing authors:
Michél C. Tigan and
Lawrence E. Clausen

ISBN 13: 978-1-59298-333-9

Library of Congress Control Number: 2010925153
Printed in the United States of America
First Printing: 2010
Second Printing: 2011
14 13 12 11 5 4 3 2

Book design by Ryan Scheife, Mayfly Design (www.mayflydesign.net)

Colorist: Ingrid Bjerstedt Rogers Ingridwarepottery@pressenter.com

Earth Images created by Artist Sue Kirchner suekirchner@mac.com from digitized photos of rock and water from northeastern and southwestern USA.

Editorial Assistance by Lisa Gagnon Sun

Beaver's Pond Press, Inc.
7104 Ohms Lane, Suite 101
Edina, MN 55439-2129
(952) 829-8818
www.BeaversPondPress.com

To order, visit www.BeaversPondBooks.com
or call (800) 901-3480. Reseller discounts available.

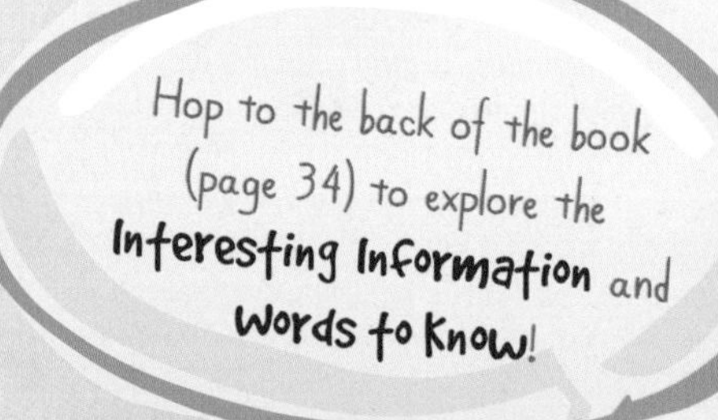

This book is dedicated with love to my parents, Bernadette and Flavian Gagnon, who taught me the importance of kindness. They embraced the challenges of life with humor, worked hard, and were always kind to their children. I miss them!

Grateful thanks for the support and encouragement of my brother Mark Gagnon and brother-in-law Monsignor William Clausen, who helped move *Green Wise Kids* to completion and beyond. A special thanks to my contributing authors, my husband Larry and our daughter Michél Tigan, who added measures of joy, knowledge, and research to the book. I thank my wonderful children, Jacqueline and Steven Graham, Brian and Candee Clausen, and Michél and Matthew Tigan for their support. I wish to thank my grandchildren: Melissa, Tony, Jennifer, Natalie, Sam, Sophie, Emelia, and Adéle; and grandnieces and grandnephews: Abby, Olivia , Claire, Liam, and Nicholas. What a grand adventure!

A special thanks for encouragement and assistance: Lisa Gagnon Sun; Elizabeth Weightman-Bragg; Mary Jo Torinus; Sue Tenner Bangert; Mary Heywood Kubiak; Vicki Edin; Ron and Martha Gagnon; Patricia Peterson; the Hudson,Wisconsin librarians Mary Davis and Carol Hardin; Kathleen Eddy; the R3 Environmental Committees of the Hudson Elementary Schools; and many other family and friends who encouraged our effort to empower one child at a time to become stewards of this wonderful planet, Earth.

Our Earth needs fixing, this is true,
So here's a special book for you.
An answer to, "What can kids do?"
Well, you've asked, so I'll tell you!
Reduce, reuse, and recycle please!
Make our Earth a better place to be.

There are other things you can do
To be **GREEN** and make
changes too!
You are noisy, joyful, and bright.
You have the power, make
things right!

Our Earth has big and small fixers.
Only small ones grace these pictures!
After reading we hope you'll say,
"Now I will live in **GREEN WISE** ways!"
So turn the page to start a new day.
Find the frogs as you walk in this
Earth-friendly way.

BOG FROGS
AND Friends 2

Green Wise

Energetic Emelia

Hudson, Wisconsin

Frogs are fun, it's plain to see.
They hop, hop, hop, just like me.
Some scientists say frogs are hopping away,
But I would like to see them stay.
I'll be kind to their earthen home
So they will have a place to roam.

If you find the home of a frog,
Do not disturb his muddy log.
Then he will have a place to stay
Where he can hop and croak all day.

Green Wise

JOYFUL JENNIFER

New Richmond, Wisconsin

If you want a song in your life every day,
A backyard birdhouse is the very best way.
Give your bird friends a drink or two,
Then they will sing all day for you.

Turn off the faucet when you are done.
Then settle in for some bird song fun!
Red birds, yellow birds, and blue ones too,
Each will sing a different song for you.

PLASTIC
BAGS
PLASTIC
BOTTLES
CANS

Green Wise

OUTSTANDING OLIVIA

Marco Island, Florida

Ocean creatures are in confusion,
Wondering the cause of pollution.
Much of our trash is filling the sea.
Cleanup is a job for you and me.

When going to school or the car,
Recycling bins are not too far.
Drop in plastic, glass, and cans you've used.
The Earth will feel much less abused.

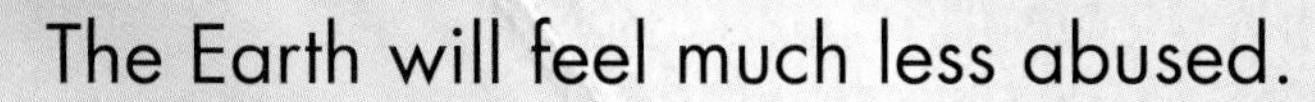

WETLAND
PRESERVE

Green Wise

Creative Claire

Hudson, Wisconsin

When hiking in parks, marshes, or bogs,
Try not to step on the sleeping frogs.
If you see a resting butterfly,
Be sure to sing a lullaby.
Worms and turtles are slow to hide,
So move your feet to the other side.

Green Wise

Marvelous Melissa

New Richmond, Wisconsin

Fly on a tire swing up to the sky,
Watch birds and butterflies flutter by.
Don't you wish you could soar so high?
A library can teach you how they fly!
To learn about creatures you pass each day
Using a library is a good way!

Green Wise

Naturalist Natalie

New Richmond, Wisconsin

You can give the Earth a great big boost!
Turn off the lights that are not in use.
Flip the switch on your way out,
Earth will smile, there is no doubt!
When going outside,
shut the door.
Keep energy inside,
that's what it's for.

Green Wise

Hudson, Wisconsin

Save the papers that you read,
They can serve another need.
Decorate bags where you can keep
Old newspapers and magazines.
You'll have quite a heap!

Ask a grown-up to help you meet
The recycle truck that comes down the street.
Hand over your papers with a smile.
They may be your new book in a while!

EARTH
Science
51

Green Wise

Lively Liam

Prior Lake, Minnesota

Bottles and cans are everywhere,
Under a bench, behind a chair.
At the park or right on the beach,
Usually they're within your reach.

So pick them up and throw them away
In a recycle bin near where you play.
Reusable bottles are a solution
To rid the world of all this pollution.

Reusable bottles save sea and land,
So always keep one close at hand.
Fill it with water, milk, or juice.
It will give you lots of use.

BRUSH
AND
DANCE
Sophie

Green Wise

Sensational Sophie

Highland Park, Minnesota

If you brush your teeth every day
A sparkling smile will come your way.
But lots of water can go down the sink.
Please turn off the water between each drink.
So much water can be used up—
It's best to always use a rinse cup.
A special cup for each of you
Would be the GREEN WISE thing to do!

Green Wise

Talented Tony

New Richmond, Wisconsin

What's happening in the ocean beneath?
Is something wrong with the coral reef?
It's hard to live in a dirty sea,
Scientists say it's acidity.

Some say our oceans are too warm below,
Let's do something before the reefs go.
Study your science, someday you'll be
Changing this ocean activity.
Until then, the best a kid can do:
Reduce, reuse, and recycle—it's all about you!

Green Wise

Scientific Sam

Highland Park, Minnesota

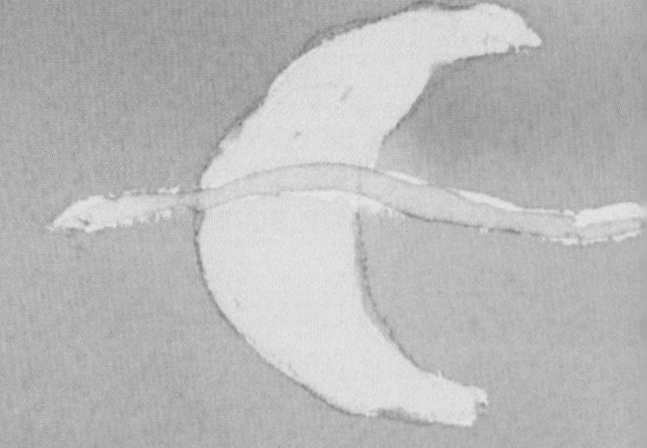

In the backyard, when it's clear,
Watch the stars both far and near.
The sky above fills the night,
Twinkling stars are the only light.

The sky will stay clear to view,
Stars and planets shining through,
If we each do a thing or two
To keep pollution out of view.

When going to work, school,
or play
Use your leg-fuel every day.
So ride your bike or walk
each way.
Show your friends the
Earth-friendly way.

A
G
B

Green Wise

Amazing Adéle

Hudson, Wisconsin

This is Adéle—she's too young to walk.
Adéle is also too young to talk.
But if she could speak, she would say,
"Plant a tree in the Earth today!"
At a picnic or a parade,
It's nice to have plenty of shade.
Trees are busy all
the day through
They make new air
for me and you!

EASY
COMPOST
WORMS

Green Wise

Nimble Nicholas

Walnut Creek, California

With your family, build a bin
Where you can throw used food scraps in.
After sometime you will find
The food is gone, soil left behind.
Now hoe a garden and plant a seed
With soil from food you didn't need.

REUSE
REDUCE
RECYCLE

Green Wise

Magical Marky

Hudson, Wisconsin

"At last," says Marky, "it's time for me
To send a message filled with glee."
Sing or whistle, it will do—
Play a violin, piano, zither, or two.
Bang on a drum or tap your knee.
The Earth is living, don't you see?

Be kind to your parents,
Your sister, and brother.
Be kind to your neighbor and cat.
Kindness brings happiness and that
is that!

We must be kind to our Earth,
rocks, and trees,
The bats, dolphins, sharks, and bees,
The rivers, streams, mountains,
and sky,
The moss, moose, and creek
flowing by,
The frogs, crickets, and bountiful sea.
It's all very important, you must see!
Important for you and for me,
It's about our Earth's ecology.
Mix this kindness with music and
it will be
A grand wish that I send to you
from me.

Interesting Information

Frog Friends

- Scientists in California say there are approximately 6,300 known *amphibian* species (like blue and orange poison dart frogs, and more). Presently, one-third of these species are vulnerable, endangered, or critically endangered.
- We can learn a great deal about the Earth from our amphibian friends because they are an *indicator species*. Indicator species are the first ones affected by environmental or habitat changes. So, for example, if we see that frogs aren't growing properly, we know that something has changed in the wetland where they live. Frogs, toads, and salamanders are highly affected by chemicals like fertilizers, weed and pest killers, and detergents released into their environment. This is because amphibians breathe and absorb water through their skin, making it easier for the chemicals to enter their bodies. Their eggs and babies are even more vulnerable to these chemicals.
- We can help our frog friends by no longer using chemicals on our lawns and buying biodegradable cleaning products for our homes. Go green for the frogs, and celebrate a dandelion or two . . . you may just feed a neighboring bunny rabbit too!

Big Birds and Song Birds

- There are about ten thousand kinds of birds of every shape and size. Birds come in all the colors of the rainbow and many sing musical songs, some even copy our words. The tiny hummingbird and the majestic condor cannot sing, but they are fun to watch. All birds lay eggs and have feathers and wings. Most use their wings to fly. But some, like ostriches and penguins, cannot fly. Like you and me, they walk and run.

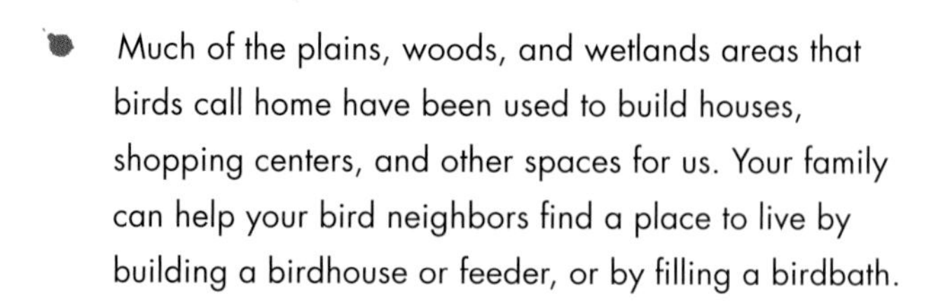

- Much of the plains, woods, and wetlands areas that birds call home have been used to build houses, shopping centers, and other spaces for us. Your family can help your bird neighbors find a place to live by building a birdhouse or feeder, or by filling a birdbath.

Stash the Trash

- A wide variety of garbage, including soda cans, plastic bottles, bags, toothbrushes, balloons, and much more, pollute our oceans, rivers, and lakes. Some of the garbage comes from storm drains and sewers as well as from picnicking and beach-going trash.
- Most of the plastic trash sinks to the ocean floor, but somewhere between San Francisco and Hawaii in the Pacific Ocean is an island of floating trash the size of the state of Texas. This is huge!
- Sea creatures often mistake this garbage for food. As many as one million sea birds and a hundred thousand ocean mammals and sea turtles die each year from eating this plastic stew.
- The trash island is not solid but more like a soup that floats just beneath the surface. This stew also leaks harmful chemicals into the seawater. Fish absorb the chemicals and eat the plastic particles, and these fish can end up on a family's dinner table! It is vital that we put an end to plastic waste! Limit your use of plastic products by using reusable items, such as water bottles, shopping bags, and lunch boxes.

Wetland Homes

- Wetlands, including swamps, marshes, and bogs, are areas of land where the soil is full of water. Wetlands are natural homes for creatures like frogs, turtles, dragonflies, as well as many others. Wetlands can be full of fresh water, salt water, or a mixture of both.

Interesting Information

- Wetlands are one of the most important of our ecosystems because they contain the largest group of different types of plants and animals working together. As human populations grow, we drain or fill in the wetlands to create farmland and to build homes, highways, and cities. At first we did not know the harm this caused to the plants and animals that lived in the wetlands or the important role the wetlands play in purifying our water.
- We now know how important it is to save our wetlands. Wetlands are the places many of our animals, birds, and insects are born. They are the giant nurseries for these wetland babies.

Birds, Butterflies, and Forests

- Every year, nearly 350 types of birds travel between their wintering grounds in South and Central America and their summer homes in North America. Many birds make their homes in the 1.5 million acres of the Northern Hemisphere's *Boreal Forest.* Unfortunately, more than 240 million acres of this forest have lost many of their trees to over-logging. That means fewer places for birds to stay as they make their journey. The numbers of northern birds, including the Evening Grosbeak, Olive-sided Flycatcher, Canada Warbler, Bay-breasted Warbler, and the Rusty Blackbird, have declined by more than 70% in the last forty years.
- Birds and butterflies make their homes in the forest in trees and meadows. Each year, 2–3 million acres of the Boreal Forest are lost to making products made from trees. By using recycled paper, you lessen the need to cut down new trees and reduce the damage to this ecosystem, the birds' and butterflies' home.

Shut Off Greenhouse Gas

- Whenever we use electricity, we put a kind of pollution called *greenhouse gases* into the air.
- We can save electricity by hooking electrical appliances (for example, lights, televisions, and computers) to a *power strip.* Use a power strip that shuts everything down at night. You use less energy and produce less greenhouse gas.
- Lightbulbs can be replaced with new, energy-saving bulbs like *compact fluorescents,* which use 75% less energy and last ten times longer!

Make "Your" New Book

- Every year Americans use an average of 700 pounds of paper products per person—that adds up to about seven trees per person, or two million trees a year. Also, about one billion trees' worth of paper are thrown away each year in the United States.
- Recycling reduces the total number of trees that are cut down to make paper. But more importantly, paper recycling saves forests. By using recycled paper (made from your old newspapers and magazines) instead of new paper made from trees, you can reduce the number of trees that are cut down each year.

Interesting Information

Use it Again

- On average, each person in the United States produces 4.4 pounds of solid waste each day. This adds up to one ton of trash per person per year. Currently about only 26% is recycled or composted.
- The boxes and packages in which we buy products make up about 33% of all our garbage.
- Aluminum and steel cans, cardboard, glass, newspapers, and plastic bottles are all recyclable and can be used to make new products. Some of the new products are small, like new bottles and cans, and some are really big, like school buses, playground equipment, and even building materials for skyscrapers.

Water is Life

- Each person in a household uses between eighty and one hundred gallons of water per day. An average household uses 350 gallons of water a day and 127,400 gallons a year. Is there a gallon of milk in your refrigerator? Imagine 350 gallon jugs lined up in your front yard. Now imagine 127,000 of them!
- Cutting down on water waste during tooth-brushing can save up to eight gallons of water per person per day. If you turn off the tap while you're brushing your teeth, you can save almost three thousand gallons of water per year. Wow! What a difference you can make.

Coral Rainbows

- Coral reefs look like big, rocky, rainbow gardens in the sea. Thousands of tiny, colorful animals called coral polyps build the reefs. Reefs are the *rain forests* of the ocean. Unfortunately, these reefs are disappearing at an alarming rate. Due to careless fishing, tourism, and boating, we may have lost as much as 50% of the world's reef-building corals.
- Some scientists believe that global warming is also contributing to the loss, due to the rise in ocean temperatures. If the ocean temperature is too high, the tiny coral animals get sick and die. Scientists also believe that pollution from sewage and farm runoff is adding to the death of the coral reefs.
- Be sure to eat only sustainably caught or harvested fish to help protect our coral reefs.

Clear Skies Up Above

- *Air pollution* can be caused by burning fuel in our cars, homes, and industries. It creates a haze or fog that is difficult to see through. Natural events such as *volcanic eruptions* and forest fires can also increase air pollution. But when humans add a lot more air pollution to this natural cycle, the trees that filter it can't keep up.
- We can all help to reduce air pollution by using mass transportation like buses, subways, and light-rail trains. We can choose to drive less and walk and bike more. The power to help our planet is in the hands of all of us. Small steps add up to big changes when we all pitch in to improve our health and the health of our Earth.

Interesting Information

Take a Deep Breath—Thanks, Trees!

- As trees grow, they make the air that we breathe. A single full-grown tree can make enough oxygen for your family for at least a year. Trees absorb *carbon dioxide,* which is one of the most harmful greenhouse gases. Scientists believe that too much greenhouse gas warms our air and may hurt our Earth by changing the weather around the world. That can also change the places animals live. This can cause big problems if you are a polar bear and all the ice you live on is melting!
- Trees also help filter our drinking water and even provide a spot for birds to nest and grasshoppers to have a tasty leaf lunch.
- Did you know that an estimated one hundred million trees are chopped down every year to make junk mail? This is the mail that flows into our homes in the form of catalogs, coupons, and more. That is way too much! The average family gets thirteen thousand pieces of junk mail per year. Your family can help by recycling paper, using reusable cloth bags, and canceling some of the junk mail that comes to your house. You can also read more as a family about how to help our beautiful trees and the planet we share. Many services are available online to stop junk mail, take a look.

Family Project: Composting

- *Compost* is easily made by recycling leftover food and other kitchen scraps. Your family can get started by throwing food scraps into a large yogurt container (or other reusable container). Orange peels, potato skins, banana peels, coffee grounds, and other fruit and vegetable bits are okay, but keep the cheese, meat, and other animal products out! Once the container is full, find a space outside for a compost bin. You can use any large container or even a bucket if you have limited space. Add grass clippings and leaves only if you don't use pesticides. Give the pile a turn and a little sprinkle of water occasionally. After just the first year, your old food scraps will have become soil that you can use to grow a tomato plant or an apple tree, or you can even mix it into your garden plot! Your plants will surely thank you, and so will the Earth, because the amount of garbage you throw into our landfills will be dramatically decreased. Good luck!
- Yard trimmings and food waste make up 26% of the U.S. municipal solid waste stream. Each person who composts saves over four hundred pounds of waste per year.

Green Wise Marky

- Children with special needs require greater access to our parks, trails and waterways. You and your family can make this a reality by volunteering and by supporting laws to improve accessibility. Encourage more outdoor opportunities for these Green Wise kids by being an advocate for their special needs.

Words to Know

Air Pollution

Harmful amounts of dust, fumes, or gases in the air. Air pollution can damage the health of plants and animals, including humans.

Amphibians

Cold-blooded animals such as frogs and toads that are born as water-breathing animals and become air-breathers as adults. Most adult amphibians have four legs.

Boreal Forest

"Boreal" means northern from the Greek god, Boreus of the North Wind. The forest is so huge it grows across Alaska, Scandinavia, and Russia. It makes up a third of the Earth's total forest area. From the Southern Hemisphere birds fly to this northern forest by the billions! This forest acts as a nursery for birds and hundreds of other plants and animals. Unfortunately, this forest is threatened by clear cut logging, moss harvesting, oil and gas extraction, dam building and other developments.

Carbon Dioxide

A colorless, odorless, unburnable gas caused by respiration (breathing), combustion (burning fuels), and organic decomposition (rotting and decaying plants and animals). Carbon dioxide is made of the chemicals oxygen and carbon. Plants take this gas in and return oxygen to the air.

Compact Fluorescents

Energy-saving light bulbs containing gases that increase the amount of light made by the bulb but decrease the amount of energy needed to run them. Compact fluorescent bulbs last much longer than other lightbulbs.

Ecology

The science of living things interacting with their environments.

Ecosystem

All of the plants, animals, minerals and people working together in any area of the Earth. For example, freshwater ecosystems are made up of lakes and rivers, the plants, fish, and insects in those bodies of water, and the humans who use the water for fishing, boating, bathing, and drinking. Other ecosystems include forests, grasslands, urban areas, and many more. Together they make up one giant ecosystem, the Earth.

Greenhouse Gases

Gases in Earth's atmosphere that absorb light and heat from the Sun and increase the temperature on Earth. Greenhouse gases are produced when substances burn. Natural sources of greenhouse gases include forest fires and volcanoes. Humans add more greenhouse gases by burning fossil fuels like coal, oil, and gasoline. Between 1906 and 2005 the Earth has become 1–1.7°F warmer. This may have a harmful effect on our world.

Indicator Species

Groups of plants or animals used to gather information about the health of their environment. When many members of an indicator species get sick or disappear, it indicates that something is wrong with the ecosystems in which these species live. An example of this might be the worldwide disappearances of frogs due to water pollution.

Ocean Acidity

ocean acidity takes place in ocean water when chemical substances like carbon dioxide (CO2), sulfur, or nitrogen mix with seawater in the form of rain or directly from the shoreline. It hurts the coastal and shallow area and organisms that live in these areas. Ocean acidity decreases the ability of some creatures like sea urchins, corals, and certain types of plankton to use calcium carbonate, which builds their protective outer shells. These creatures are important in the marine food chain because they provide food and habitat to other species. They are the base of ocean ecosystems and impact our food chain dramatically. It is believed that if current rates continue, by the end of this century ocean acidity will be five times greater than today. We can stop this increase by decreasing pollution draining into our oceans from stream, rivers, and rainfall.

Power Strips

Strips of power sockets attached to flexible power cables. Power strips allow multiple electrical devices to be turned on or shut off at the same time. They can stop power loss from appliances and save electricity.

Rain Forests

Lush, evergreen forests with yearly rainfalls of at least 160 inches. Rain forests are often, but not always, located in tropical areas. The Amazon region in South America makes up one half of our planet's rain forests.

Volcanic Eruptions

Explosions of dust, gas, ashes, and lava from beneath Earth's surface. A volcano is a hole in Earth's crust that opens down to a pool of molten rock, or magma. When the pieces of Earth's crust shift, magma can burst through this hole and release greenhouse gases along with lava and ashes.

Further Resources

Websites

The Enviro-Link Network: http://www.envirolink.org/ Find links to thousands of online environmental resources.

EPA Environmental Kids Club: http://www.epa.gov/kids/ Learn about our environment and ways to protect it through games, stories, and art projects.

Zipper's Green Tips (*National Geographic Kids*): http://wwwkids.nationalgeographic.com/ Read about easy ways to protect our planet, and then explore the rest of the *National Geographic Kids* website.

EcoKids: http://www.ecokids.ca/pub/kids_home.cfm Play games and read the news from kid EcoReporters across North America.

Kids F.A.C.E. (Kids for a Clean Environment): http://www.kidsface.org/ Find news and information about saving the Earth at the world's largest youth environmental organization.

Defenders of Wildlife (Kids Planet): http://kidsplanet.org Read about the Web of Life and learn how to defend wildlife in your area at this kid-focused site.

The Monterey Bay Aquarium http://www.montereybayaquarium.org/cr/seafoodwatch.aspx.

The Marine Stewardship Council: http://www.msc.org/ Buy only sustainable seafood certified by the Marine Stewardship Council.

Books for Kids, Parents, and Teachers

The Down-To-Earth Guide to Global Warming by Laurie David and Cambria Gordon (New York, NY: Orchard Books, 2007)

Endangered Animals, Volumes 1–10 (Danbury, CT: Grolier Educational, 2001)

Garbage and Recycling, by Helen Orme (New York, NY: Bearport Publishing, 2008)

One Tree, by Leslie Bockol (Norwalk, CT: innovativekids, 2009)

Pollution by Helen Orme (New York, NY: Bearport Publishing, 2008)

Reducing and Recycling Waste by Carol Inskipp (Milwaukee, WI: Gareth Stevens Publishing, 2005)

Trash and Recycling by Stephanie Turnbull (London, UK: Usborne Publishing, 2006)

Why Are the Ice Caps Melting? by Anne Rockwell (New York, NY: HarperCollins, 2006)

Worms Eat My Garbage: How to Set Up and Maintain a Worm Composting System, by Mary Appelhof (Kalamazoo, MI: Flower Press, 1997)

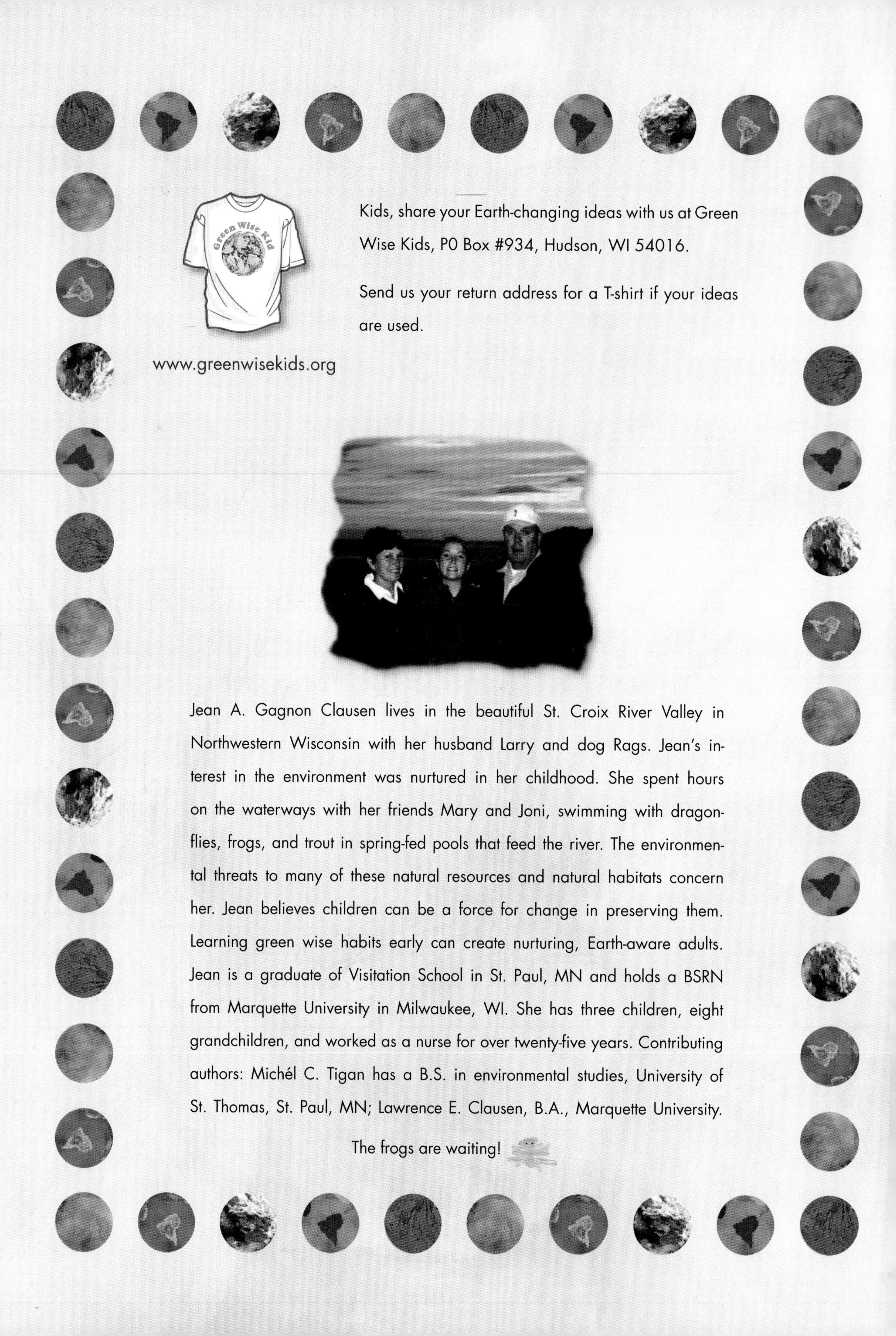

Kids, share your Earth-changing ideas with us at Green Wise Kids, PO Box #934, Hudson, WI 54016.

Send us your return address for a T-shirt if your ideas are used.

www.greenwisekids.org

Jean A. Gagnon Clausen lives in the beautiful St. Croix River Valley in Northwestern Wisconsin with her husband Larry and dog Rags. Jean's interest in the environment was nurtured in her childhood. She spent hours on the waterways with her friends Mary and Joni, swimming with dragonflies, frogs, and trout in spring-fed pools that feed the river. The environmental threats to many of these natural resources and natural habitats concern her. Jean believes children can be a force for change in preserving them. Learning green wise habits early can create nurturing, Earth-aware adults. Jean is a graduate of Visitation School in St. Paul, MN and holds a BSRN from Marquette University in Milwaukee, WI. She has three children, eight grandchildren, and worked as a nurse for over twenty-five years. Contributing authors: Michél C. Tigan has a B.S. in environmental studies, University of St. Thomas, St. Paul, MN; Lawrence E. Clausen, B.A., Marquette University.

The frogs are waiting!